Rainbow Street

by Lynne Rickards and Marie-Rose Boisson

W
FRANKLIN WATTS
LONDON • SYDNEY

Chapter 1

Samir woke up early. It was a bright, sunny morning on Rainbow Street, but his brother Ali was still sound asleep. Samir went to open the window, as he did every morning, to greet the birds.

"Good morning, little birds," he said to the sparrows outside, holding some food out to them. One of the little sparrows was very brave and hopped up on to his hand. Samir loved birds. He thought they were the most beautiful creatures in the world.

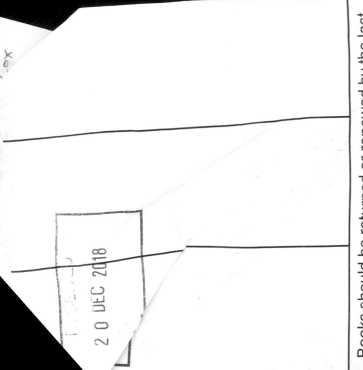

Books should be returned or renewed by the last date above. Renew by phone **03000 41 31 31** or online *www.kent.gov.uk/libs*

Samir quickly woke his brother Ali.

The boys ate their breakfast in

the kitchen with Gran.

"Hurry up now," she said,

"the school bus will be here soon."

"Samir is the slow one," Ali teased.

"He's the reason we're always late. He has to

make sure all the birds get their breakfast."

"They're hungry in the morning, too," said Samir.

"They want breakfast, just like us."

The boys grabbed their school bags and raced down the stairs. The yellow bus was waiting at the bottom of Rainbow Street. They had to hurry. It wouldn't wait forever!

Samir flapped his arms and flew like a bird down the last two steps.
"I wish I had real wings," he said.
"Then I would fly to school and never be late."

Chapter 2

After school, Samir and Ali walked down
Rainbow Street to their apartment.
Gran was waiting outside for them.
"What have you got there?" she asked Samir.
He was pulling something big from his school
bag. "It's a book about birds," he said.
"My teacher gave it to me. I chose to write
about birds for my homework."
That doesn't surprise me!" laughed Gran.
"Let's have a look at it together."

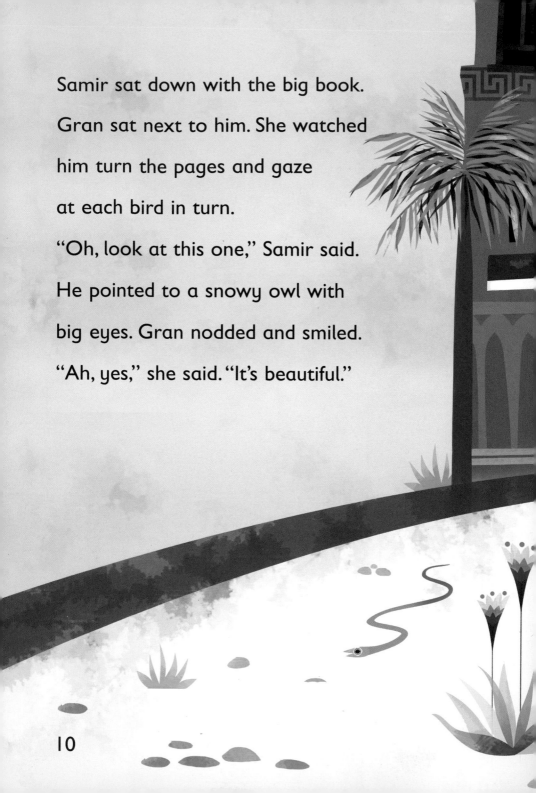

Samir sat down with the big book.
Gran sat next to him. She watched
him turn the pages and gaze
at each bird in turn.

"Oh, look at this one," Samir said.
He pointed to a snowy owl with
big eyes. Gran nodded and smiled.
"Ah, yes," she said. "It's beautiful."

On the next page was a picture of a huge falcon. It was the most amazing bird Samir had ever seen.

"My father had a falcon like that many years ago," said Gran. "He called her Aida and took her out into the desert to hunt."

"Your father was so lucky!" said Samir. "I'd do anything to have a bird like that!"

"Maybe one day, Samir," smiled Gran.

Chapter 3

The next day after school, Samir and Ali

were feeling hungry. They walked up Rainbow

Street to the bakery. Samir was still thinking

about the falcon in the book.

"Hello, boys," said the man at the counter.

"What can I get for you today?"

"I would like something sweet," said Ali.

He pointed to some sweet pastries.

Samir picked three Bird's Nest sweets.

The man put them in a little bag for him.

"Bird's Nest sweets again, Samir,"

the shopkeeper laughed.

14

At the top of Rainbow Street was a little park. Samir and Ali walked up the hill. The air was hot and dry. They passed lots of busy cafes and shops. Samir found it hard to keep up with his big brother. "Slow down, Ali," he panted.

When they reached the park, Samir was glad to sit down. At last he could eat his Bird's Nest sweets.

Chapter 4

Samir sat in the shade of a tall cypress tree.

He loved this park that looked out over the city.

On the opposite hill stood the ruins of an ancient

Roman temple.

Samir looked up. He imagined a beautiful

falcon flying high above them,

graceful and majestic, like the one

Gran had told him about.

"Look," whispered Ali.

A little sparrow had hopped next to them.

Slowly, Samir put down a Birds Nest sweet.

The sparrow hopped closer to peck at the nuts.

"He likes it," Samir whispered.

He sat very still to watch the sparrow eat.

Chapter 5

On Saturday, there was no school.
Samir and his Gran went shopping for fruit
and vegetables in Rainbow Street. They bought
oranges, cucumbers, grapes and a melon.

Samir helped his Gran with the heavy bags.
It was lucky their apartment was downhill.
Samir pretended to be a bird. He held out
one arm, like a wing, to glide home.

23

"What kind of bird are you today, Samir?"

asked Gran.

"I am a falcon," he answered.

"Ah, like Aida?" asked Gran.

"Yes, the one your father had," Samir said.

"I would love to hunt with a falcon.

Maybe one day I'll have one too."

This gave Gran an idea.

Later that day, Gran went back out to Rainbow Street. Halfway up the hill was a special market. It was called the Souk Jara. People sold crafts and artwork under shaded stalls. Gran looked at all the stalls. She walked around the whole market.

At last she found the perfect thing for Samir. She couldn't wait to see his face when she gave him his special gift ...

27

What a wonderful surprise! Samir had finally got a falcon all of his own. His wish had come true, thanks to Gran! His beautiful falcon kite flew high over the city in a pastel pink sky, flapping about beneath the setting sun.

29

Things to think about

1. How does Samir show that he likes birds?
2. What characteristics would you use to describe Samir?
3. What do you discover about Samir's daily life in Rainbow Street? How does it compare to where you live?
4. What does Gran do to surprise Samir?
5. How do you think Samir feels at the end of the story?

Write it yourself

One of the themes in this story is discovering what inspires you. Now try to write your own story with a similar theme.

Plan your story before you begin to write it.
Start off with a story map:
• a beginning to introduce the characters and where your story is set (the setting);
• a problem which the main characters will need to fix in the story;
• an ending where the problems are resolved.

Get writing! Try to use interesting descriptions with alliteration such as "pastel pink sky" to describe your story world and excite your reader.

Notes for parents and carers

Independent reading

The aim of independent reading is to read this book with ease. This series is designed to provide an opportunity for your child to read for pleasure and enjoyment. These notes are written for you to help your child make the most of this book.

About the book

Samir and his brother Ali live in a vibrant place known as Rainbow Street, in Amman, Jordan. Samir loves all things to do with birds and is desperate to own a falcon one day. His Gran has an idea that will help Samir's dream come true, at least in part, when she finds a kite in the shape of a falcon.

Before reading

Ask your child why they have selected this book. Look at the title and blurb together. What do they think it will be about? Do they think they will like it?

During reading

Encourage your child to read independently. If they get stuck on a longer word, remind them that they can find syllable chunks that can be sounded out from left to right. They can also read on in the sentence and think about what would make sense.

After reading

Support comprehension by talking about the story. What happened?
Then help your child think about the messages in the book that go beyond the story, using the questions on the page opposite. Give your child a chance to respond to the story, asking:
Did you enjoy the story and why?
Who was your favourite character?

Franklin Watts
First published in Great Britain in 2018
by The Watts Publishing Group

Series Editors: Jackie Hamley and Melanie Palmer
Series Advisors: Dr Sue Bodman and Glen Franklin
Series Designer: Peter Scoulding

A CIP catalogue record for this book is
available from the British Library.

ISBN 978 1 4451 6298 0 (hbk)
ISBN 978 1 4451 6300 0 (pbk)
ISBN 978 1 4451 6299 7 (library ebook)

Printed in China

Franklin Watts
An imprint of
Hachette Children's Group
Part of The Watts Publishing Group
Carmelite House
50 Victoria Embankment
London EC4Y 0DZ

An Hachette UK Company
www.hachette.co.uk

www.franklinwatts.co.uk

FSC
www.fsc.org
MIX
Paper from
responsible sources
FSC® C104740

Flyi
C33482
Renewa

The boy w
C334682282

Giraffe is
C334913727

How Koala got a
C334793574

Tom's

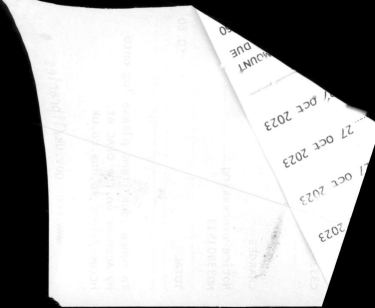

astic Mr Fox

C=3C4J686

CHARGES

tire processing

W=335J151

Notes for parents and carers

Independent reading

The aim of independent reading is to read this book with ease. This series is designed to provide an opportunity for your child to read for pleasure and enjoyment. These notes are written for you to help your child make the most of this book.

About the book

Samir and his brother Ali live in a vibrant place known as Rainbow Street, in Amman, Jordan. Samir loves all things to do with birds and is desperate to own a falcon one day. His Gran has an idea that will help Samir's dream come true, at least in part, when she finds a kite in the shape of a falcon.

Before reading

Ask your child why they have selected this book. Look at the title and blurb together. What do they think it will be about? Do they think they will like it?

During reading

Encourage your child to read independently. If they get stuck on a longer word, remind them that they can find syllable chunks that can be sounded out from left to right. They can also read on in the sentence and think about what would make sense.

After reading

Support comprehension by talking about the story. What happened? Then help your child think about the messages in the book that go beyond the story, using the questions on the page opposite. Give your child a chance to respond to the story, asking:

Did you enjoy the story and why?

Who was your favourite character?

Franklin Watts
First published in Great Britain in 2018
by The Watts Publishing Group

Series Editors: Jackie Hamley and Melanie Palmer
Series Advisors: Dr Sue Bodman and Glen Franklin
Series Designer: Peter Scoulding

A CIP catalogue record for this book is
available from the British Library.

ISBN 978 1 4451 6298 0 (hbk)
ISBN 978 1 4451 6300 0 (pbk)
ISBN 978 1 4451 6299 7 (library ebook)

Printed in China

Franklin Watts
An imprint of
Hachette Children's Group
Part of The Watts Publishing Group
Carmelite House
50 Victoria Embankment
London EC4Y 0DZ

An Hachette UK Company
www.hachette.co.uk

www.franklinwatts.co.uk

FSC
www.fsc.org
MIX
Paper from
responsible sources
FSC® C104740